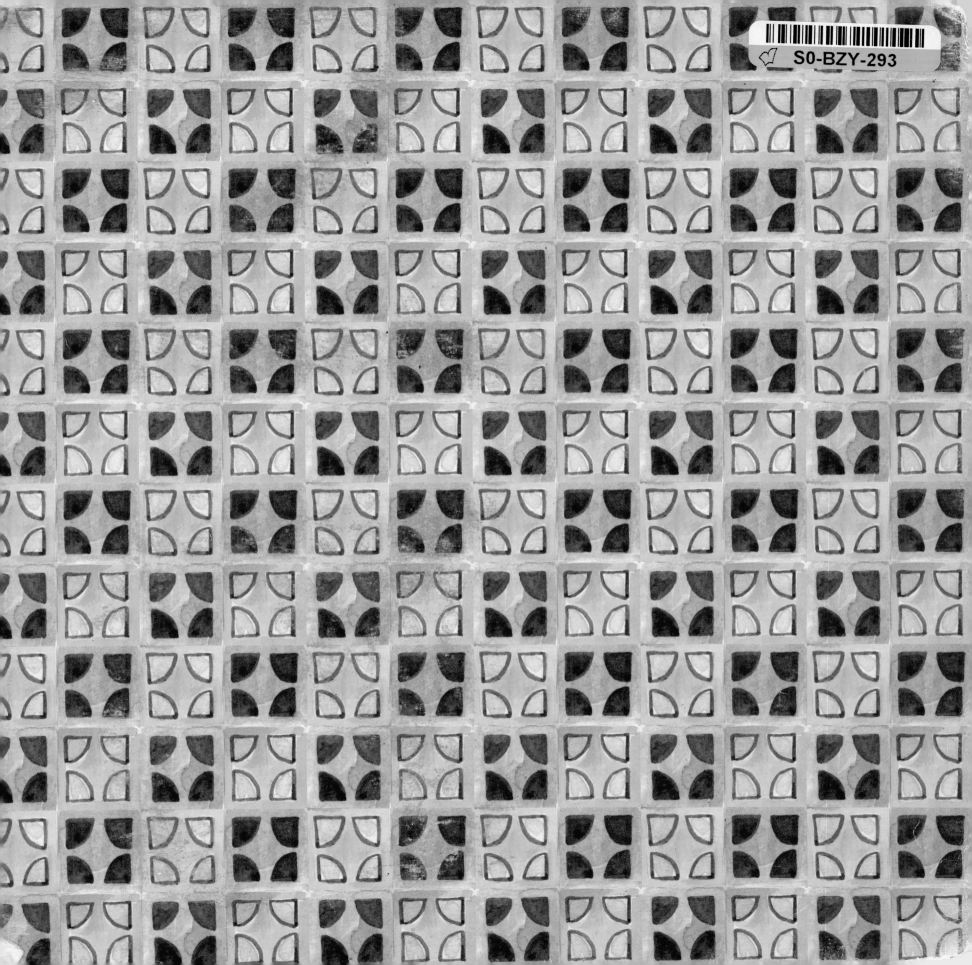

For
Grandad Burns and Grandad Roberts
and to the memory of
Nana Jean Burns and
Grandma Anne "Queenie" Roberts

Rapunzel

a groovy fairy tale

RETOLD BY
Lynn Roberts

ILLUSTRATED BY
David Roberts

In a time not too long ago and in a land much like our own, there lived a very beautiful girl with the most extraordinarily long red hair.

Her name was Rapunzel, and she lived with her Aunt Esme and Roach, Esme's hideous pet crow. Rapunzel had been brought up by Esme after her parents died when she was very young. Esme kept her locked up so she could not go out and enjoy herself.

To keep Rapunzel quiet (and to make herself seem nice, which she was not) Esme brought Rapunzel second-hand magazines and records and occasionally allowed her to watch television. "When you are older," Esme lied, "I'll take you out and show you the city, but it's not safe for you on your own."

Rapunzel believed every word, for she knew nothing of the world.

The apartment building they lived in was old and deserted. The elevator was always broken, and there were hundreds of stairs to the ground. This was not a problem for Aunt Esme because she had a special way of entering and leaving the building.

Rapunzel would hang her braid over the balcony and Esme would climb down it. On her return she would shout, "Rapunzel, Rapunzel, let down your hair!" Then, Rapunzel would throw her long braid over the balcony, Esme would grab hold, and Rapunzel would slowly pull her up.

Aunt Esme worked at the local school. She was the most fearsome lunch lady the children had ever seen. Prowling around the cafeteria, she would force them to eat every scrap of food, even cold pea soup and lumpy pudding. Esme also trained Roach to swoop down and steal things from the children to bring to her. Esme selfishly took all the best things and gave the scarves and jewelry she did not like to Rapunzel, pretending she had bought them.

One morning, as Aunt Esme struggled down Rapunzel's hair, a boy who had stopped to fix his bike on the way to school happened to see this extraordinary sight. His name was Roger, and he was the singer in the local school band, Roger and the Rascals. As Aunt Esme roared off on her motorcycle, he thought "That's the nasty lunch lady from school! What is she doing?"

After school he raced back to the apartment. To his astonishment he heard the nasty lunch lady booming out, "Rapunzel, Rapunzel, let down your hair!" Seeing the beautiful red braid tumble over the balcony, Roger knew he had to meet the girl with the long hair.

The next day was Saturday, and Roger could not wait to go back. Luckily for him, Esme was just on her way to a fitness class.

Roger took a deep breath, and trying his best to imitate Esme's booming voice, he called, "Rapunzel, Rapunzel, let down your hair!" To his amazement, the rope of hair was lowered. Hesitantly Roger took hold of it, then gasped as he was lifted instantly into the air.

When he reached the balcony, he fell over the wall onto all fours. "Oh my!" Rapunzel exclaimed as she found herself face-to-face with the most handsome boy she had ever seen.

Rapunzel and Roger spent the whole morning listening to music and talking. "I feel as if I've known you forever," Rapunzel whispered, gazing into Roger's eyes.

Every day after this Roger would wait for Esme to leave and then visit Rapunzel to say good morning before he went to school. He took Rapunzel a present every lunchtime, and sometimes he took along his guitar so he could sing his new songs for her. She was happier than she had ever been.

One day Roger said, "I wish I could find a way to get you out of the apartment so that I could show you the city. You cannot very well climb down your own hair. And we cannot take the stairs as Esme never forgets to lock the door." Rapunzel thought for a moment. "I have a great idea!" she said. "Why don't we make a rope ladder from all the scarves and belts I have?"

Together they set to work.

The very next day, after saying good-bye to Roger, Rapunzel let down her hair for her aunt. As Esme reached the top, Rapunzel said without thinking, "You are so heavy, Aunt. It is so much easier to pull up my dear Roger."

The moment the words were out, Rapunzel knew she had spoiled everything.

Esme flew into a rage. She grabbed a pair of scissors and cut off Rapunzel's long hair. "How dare you deceive me?" cried Esme as she forced Rapunzel to climb down her own hair. "May you never find happiness!" she screamed. Seething with anger, Esme waited on the balcony for Roger.

Before long Roger called to Rapunzel to let down her hair and whistled as he was lifted up, happy at the thought of seeing her again.

But to his horror, when he reached the top, the ugly, twisted face of Esme leered out at him. "You will never see Rapunzel again," Esme hissed in his ear as she pushed him backward over the balcony. The hair tumbled with him as he fell to the ground. Wrapped around him, the braid broke his fall, but he banged his head and fell unconscious.

Meanwhile, wandering through the city streets, Rapunzel grew tired and hungry. She found a stray kitten nearly as hungry as she was and called him Rascal after Roger's band. All her life she had wanted to visit the city, but never had she felt more lonely and lost. "Will I ever see Roger again?" she wondered, holding Rascal close.

Roger, however, remembered nothing about
Rapunzel. Dazed from his fall, he staggered home
with the hair he had found wrapped around his
body. He had no idea where it had come from.
Roger put it in his dad's garage, which he used as
a studio. "It must mean something," he thought,
as he practiced his guitar.

Rapunzel slept in a damp shop doorway that night with Rascal clasped in her arms. As she awoke, stretching her arms and yawning, she caught sight of a poster. "Roger!" she cried out in surprise. Her beloved Roger and his band were playing a concert at the school that very evening. She would find the school and see Roger again!

Rapunzel could barely contain her excitement when she arrived for the concert. She found a space in the front row just as Roger and his band walked onstage to loud applause. Roger looked out into the crowd, and as he began to sing, his eyes rested on a strangely familiar halo of red hair. And when he looked at Rapunzel's beautiful, smiling face, he remembered everything.

Rapunzel and Roger were best friends from that moment on and as happy as could be. Roger and the Rascals became very successful, playing at every school in town. Rapunzel, deciding to make use of her glorious red hair, learned how to make wigs. She designed them in every style and length imaginable, as long as they were red!

And what happened to Aunt Esme? Well, she no longer had

Rapunzel's hair, and the elevator was, of course, out of order....

Illustrator's Note

When I was asked to illustrate a second fairy tale (my first being *Cinderella: An Art Deco Love Story*),
I was very keen to do the story of Rapunzel. At my sister's suggestion, I decided to set the story in a 1970s
apartment block, the obvious association with the 1970s being Rapunzel's long hair. As a child growing up
at that time, I was very influenced by the music, films, fashion, and design of the period. In researching this
book, I looked at old family photos and magazines to help me remember the clothes and toys I had owned as a
child. I have incorporated record sleeves, film posters, furniture, and product design from this period into my
illustrations. I also wanted to link Cinderella to Rapunzel in a subtle way. I imagined the families to be related,
and so a few artifacts from *Cinderella* have been passed down and found their way into Rapunzel's home.

Designer: Roger Daniels

The illustrations were done in pen and ink with watercolor on hot-pressed, heavyweight paper.

Conceived and produced by Breslich & Foss Ltd., London

Library of Congress Cataloging-in-Publication Data

Roberts, Lynn (Lynn M.)
Rapunzel : a groovy fairy tale / retold by Lynn Roberts ; illustrated
by David Roberts.
p. cm.
Summary: In this updated version of the Grimm fairy tale, Rapunzel has
flaming red hair and is kept imprisoned by her Aunt Esme, a heartless
school cafeteria worker, in a tenement apartment with a broken elevator.

ISBN 0-8109-4242-9
[1. Fairy tales. 2. Folklore--Germany.] I. Roberts, David, 1970- ill.
II. Rapunzel. English. III. Title.

PZ8.R52 Rap 2003
398.2--dc21

2002011723

Printed and bound in China

10 9 8 7 6 5 4 3 2 1

Harry N. Abrams, Inc.
100 Fifth Avenue
New York, N.Y. 10011
www.abramsbooks.com

Abrams is a subsidiary of

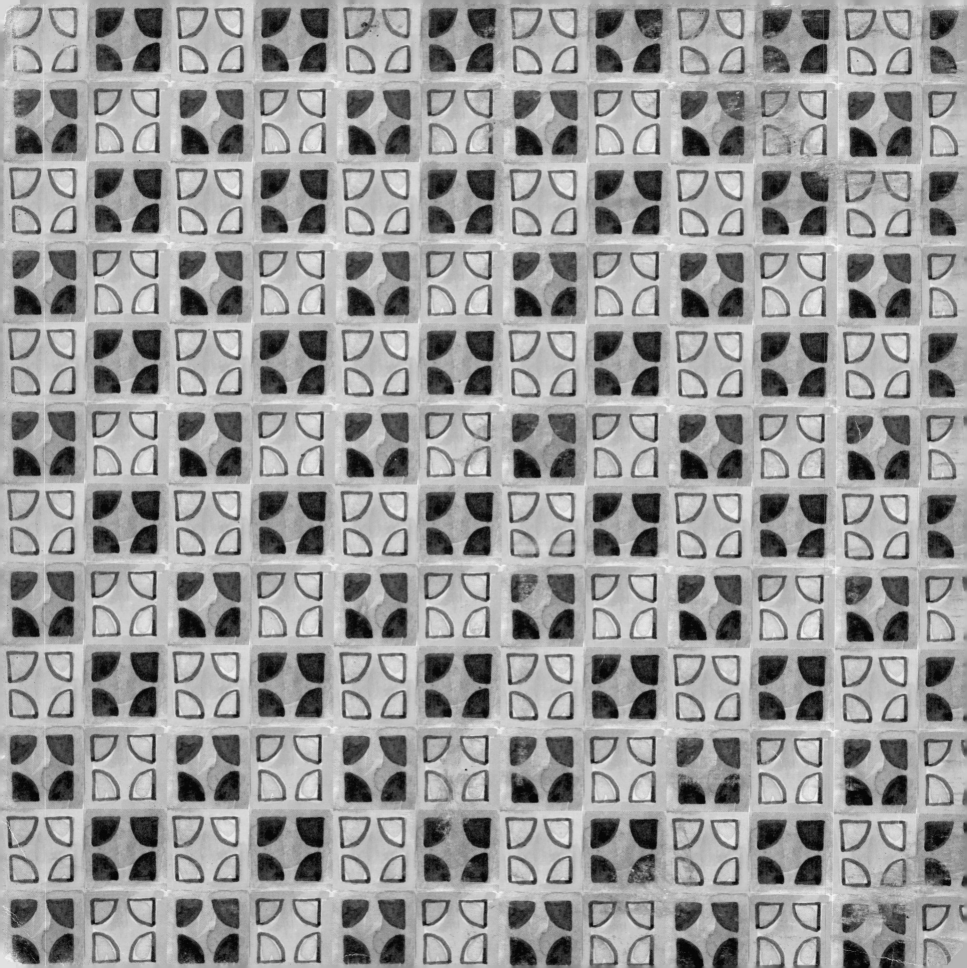